Brianna Breathes Easy

A Story about Asthma

Virginia Kroll

illustrated by Jayoung Cho

Albert Whitman & Company, Morton Grove, Illinois

With love to my friend, Jane Herman, who helps me breathe easy—V.K.

To Joowon and Jungyill and all of my family—J.C.

Library of Congress
Cataloging-in-Publication Data

Kroll, Virginia L.
Brianna breathes easy : a story about asthma /
by Virginia Kroll ; illustrated by Jayoung Cho.
p. cm.
Summary: Brianna is excited about playing the lead in her
school's Thanksgiving play, but when a terrible coughing fit sends
her to the emergency room the Friday before the show, she
learns that she has asthma and how to control it.
ISBN 0-8075-0880-2 (hardcover)
(1. Asthma—Fiction. 2. Theater—Fiction.
3. Schools—Fiction. 4. Thanksgiving Day—
Fiction.) I. Cho, Jayoung, ill. II. Title.
PZ7.K9227Br 2005 (E)—dc22 2004018642

The design is by Carol Gildar.

For more information about Albert Whitman & Company, please visit our web site at www.albertwhitman.com.

Note

Two of my children, a granddaughter, and I all have asthma. Thanks to the ongoing care of Dr. Herman and our medications, we all have the disease under control, and we're breathing easy. V.K.

Asthma is a disease that affects breathing. When an asthma attack occurs, the muscles surrounding the airways tighten and thick mucus forms, making it difficult for air to pass through. Serious asthma attacks can require treatment in a hospital, and if not properly treated, asthma can cause permanent damage to the lungs. Asthma in children is on the rise worldwide, and in the United States it is the leading chronic illness of childhood, resulting in many visits to the emergency room and absences from school.

Although the cause of asthma is not known, we do know that certain "triggers" can set off an attack. Common triggers include allergens such as pollen, pet dander, dust mites, molds, and some foods. Viral infections, irritants (smoke, pollution, and cold air), physical exertion, or emotional stress can cause airways to constrict, too. While some people have asthma attacks regardless of triggers, avoiding the triggers whenever possible is a good way to head off trouble.

While there is no cure yet, asthma can be successfully managed so that children and adults can live long and active lives, even playing sports. There are many safe and effective asthma medications. Staying on a treatment plan that has been set up especially for you by your doctor or health care provider will help you avoid flare-ups and "breathe easy."

Steven P. Herman, M.D.

"Mama, Daddy!" Brianna called, running into the house. "I got the lead in the Thanksgiving play! Mrs. Mallard wants a good dancer with a strong voice, so she picked me. I'm Hero the Hen! I save the whole flock of turkeys from Farmer Fritter."

Brianna was talking so fast that she coughed and sputtered. Mama hugged her and said, "Slow down. Take a breath between words, will you?"

"Hey, are you okay?" asked Brianna's sister, Sierra.

"You okay?" her little brother, Darrell, repeated.

"Yeah, fine," Brianna said when she could finally take a breath without coughing.

"Whew!" sighed Mama and Daddy together.

After dinner, Brianna asked, "Can I go tell Grampy about the play?"

"Sure," said Mama. "But don't stay too long. Friday's his card-playing night."

Brianna and Sierra crunched through October's fallen leaves, down the block to Grampy's house. They said hi to Mr. Morton and Mr. Wozniak, and Brianna told them all her good news.

Grampy hugged her and said, "I'll be there in that auditorium, first row." His shirt smelled like smoke. Brianna wrinkled up her nose. Grampy had never been a smoker, but Mr. Morton and Mr. Wozniak were puffing away, and a gray fog had settled over the room.

Brianna said goodbye and coughed all the way down the block.

"Maybe you'd better stay home from school tomorrow, Bri," Sierra said as they walked into the house. "You might be getting sick."

"I can't," Brianna whined. "Play rehearsals start tomorrow."

Mama agreed with Sierra. "You have been coughing a lot lately," Mama said.

But by bedtime, Brianna was feeling fine and fit as ever, so Mama said she could go to school after all.

For the next few weeks, rehearsals were fun, and the play was shaping up nicely. Brianna practiced leaping, flapping, and gobbling like a turkey. She worked hard at memorizing every line.

Sierra trimmed Brianna's "turkey" tee-shirt with the white feather boa she had worn to last year's prom. "There, now you'll really stand out from the flock."

Brianna's yellow felt beak fit just right, and she liked how her red neck wattles wiggled whenever she moved.

The Friday before the play, Brianna and her class took their costumes to school for the dress rehearsal. They practiced extra-well. Brianna "flew" extra-high and squawked extra-loud.

Right at the part where Hero was fooling Farmer Fritter, the fire alarm sounded!

Mrs. Mallard herded them all quickly outside.

A fire engine roared in, lights flashing and siren screeching. Everyone shivered in the frosty November air until Fire Chief Alvarez announced, "All clear. Sorry—just some dust in the cafeteria smoke alarm."

The children took their places back onstage, glad to be warm again.

The music began. Brianna felt a tightness in her chest. As soon as she took her first leap, she was gripped by the worst coughing fit ever.

She couldn't take a deep breath in. She couldn't push air out, either. Her breathing came in a raspy whistle. Mrs Mallard dashed to the phone, then ran up to Brianna. "Brianna, are you all right?" she said.

Brianna couldn't answer, and the worried look on her teacher's face made her feel even more frightened. Ms. Salvo, the school nurse, ran down the aisle. "I called 911," she said, "The ambulance is on its way."

By the time the paramedics arrived, Brianna's coughing had eased. She could breathe better, but her chest still hurt. "Wow, that was scary!" she said. "Do I have to go to the hospital?"

"I think you should," Ms. Salvo said. "We have to be sure you're okay."

The paramedics strapped Brianna onto a stretcher, put her into the ambulance, and took her to the hospital.

When Mama and Daddy rushed into the emergency room, Brianna was using a machine called a nebulizer to help her breathe. Dr. Anderson examined her, ordered blood tests, then had lots of questions.

"That's one way of putting it," Dr. Anderson said.

She showed Brianna a diagram of the body's breathing parts, called the respiratory system.

"Asthma happens when something irritates your breathing tubes," she explained. "Your body sends out chemicals that pinch those tubes together. When that happens, it's hard to get air in and out of your lungs."

"Real hard!" Brianna said.

"Well, Brianna," the doctor said at last, "you have asthma. Do you know what that is?"

"A bad way of breathing, right?" Brianna answered.

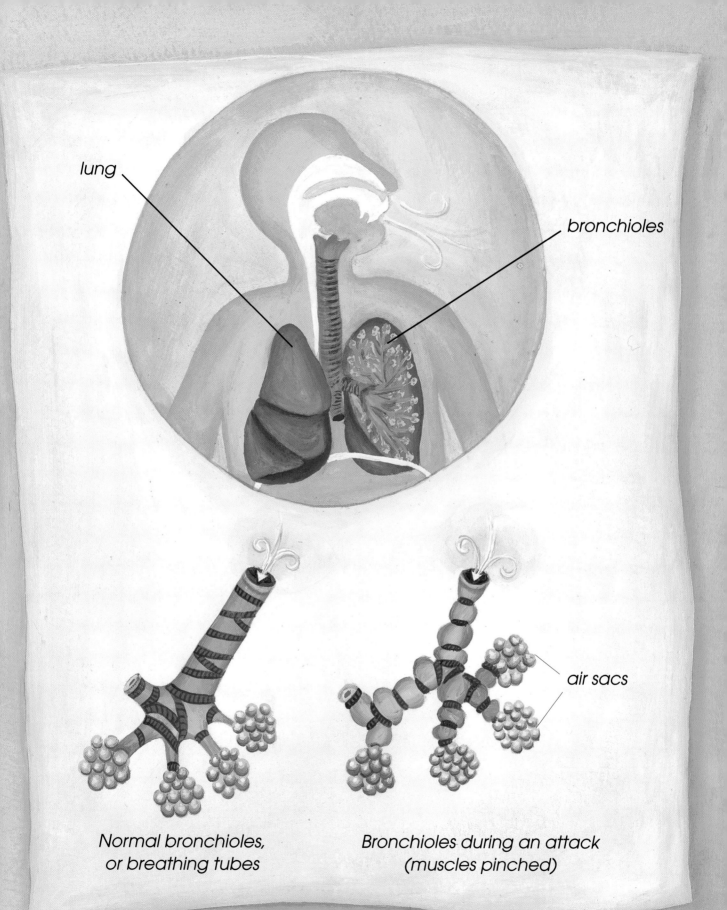

lung

bronchioles

air sacs

Normal bronchioles,
or breathing tubes

Bronchioles during an attack
(muscles pinched)

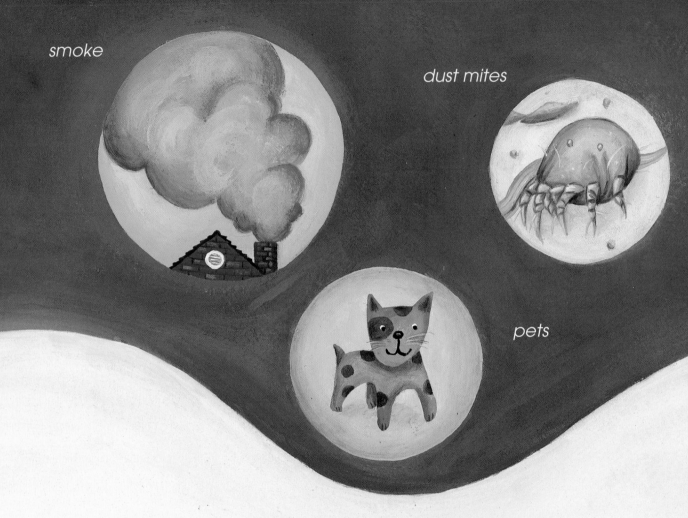

smoke

dust mites

pets

Dr. Anderson continued. "The things that bother your breathing tubes are called triggers. There are several common ones—cold weather, exercise, even being upset or excited. Some foods can do it, and inhaling certain substances, like smoke, pet dander, pollen, or even dust, which contains tiny, nasty critters called dust mites. Having a cold or the flu can make it worse, too."

Dr. Anderson asked Brianna's parents. "Do you smoke?"

"No way," they said.

Brianna told Dr. Anderson about Grampy's foggy house on card-playing night. Dr. Anderson frowned.

emotional stress

exercise

cold or flu

cold weather

Then Brianna asked,
"Is there a cure for asthma?"

"Not yet," Dr. Anderson said. "But here's the good news. You still have to be careful of the triggers, but in most cases, we can control asthma. I'm going to show you how."

"Good," Brianna said.

Dr. Anderson gave Brianna a "peak flow" meter and showed her how to blow into it. "It's like a traffic light," she explained. "When your breathing is in the green zone, you're doing okay. If it's in the yellow zone, you might need some extra medication or a nebulizer. The red zone means you're in trouble, and you need to come to the hospital right away."

Dr. Anderson gave Brianna an inhaler and showed her how to use that, too. Then she wrote out a prescription. "If you check your peak flow meter and take your medicine if you need it, Brianna, you can do all the things you like to do—except visit your grandpa when his smoking friends are over."

Daddy dropped Mama and Brianna off at home and went right to the drugstore to get her prescription filled.

On Monday morning, Brianna breathed into her peak flow meter. She used her inhaler and took her medicine at breakfast time.

Mama filled out paperwork for the school nurse's office.

At school, Michael said, "So, did you learn your colors yet, Brianna?"

Brianna frowned. "I knew all my colors way before kindergarten."

"He means your 'asthma colors,'" Yasmin said.

"Oh yeah, I'm green today," Brianna told her.

"Me, too," said Yasmin.

Brianna and Yasmin were on the same kind of medicine and had the same type of inhaler.

"You two are lucky," Michael said. "I have two inhalers, and I've got to use my nebulizer a few times every week. But I'm much better than I used to be."

Two days later, Brianna (that is, Hero the Hen!) didn't miss a leap or a gobble as she saved her Thanksgiving flock from Farmer Fritter.

Her whole family sat in front, clapping till their palms were sore.

After the play, Grampy said, "I bought ice cream and plenty of fixings. What do you say we have sundaes to celebrate?"

The kids cheered, and Darrell said, "Race you to Grampy's house."

They all took off like lightning.

Brianna got there first. Grampy had put signs on his door. There was a crossed-out cigarette in a circle, and underneath a sign that said,

Smoke-free zone—No puffing allowed!

When Grampy caught up, Brianna hugged him. "Grampy, thanks a million!" she said. She was happy he smelled like Grampy again.

"So, Hero the Hen, how are you feeling after all that squawking, talking, leaping, gobbling—and running here so fast?"

"Breathing real easy, Grampy," Brianna
said. "And it feels soooooooooo good!"